Now You Can

Read to Yourself

Now You Can
Read to Yourself

Easy-to-Read Stories selected by the

Child Study Association

of America

Illustrated by Peter Burchard

Thomas Y. Crowell Company / New York

Grateful acknowledgment is made to the following publishers for permission to reprint copyrighted matter in this book:

ABINGDON PRESS: *Andy and Mr. Wagner* by Gina Bell, copyright © 1957 by Abingdon Press; *Stevie Finds a Way* by Ruth Liebers and Lillian Rothenberg, copyright © 1955, 1958 by Abingdon Press.

THOMAS Y. CROWELL COMPANY: *What the Moon Is Like* by Franklyn M. Branley, copyright © 1963 by Franklyn M. Branley.

DOUBLEDAY & COMPANY, INC.: *Tim Tadpole and the Great Bullfrog* by Marjorie Flack, copyright © 1934 by Marjorie Flack Larsson. Reprinted by permission of Doubleday & Company, Inc.

GOLDEN PRESS, INC.: *Too Many Bozos* by Lilian Moore, copyright © 1960 by Golden Press, Inc.

HOLIDAY HOUSE: *Peep-Lo* by Jane Castle, copyright © 1959 by Holiday House.

ALFRED A. KNOPF, INC.: *The Silver Button* by Helen D. Olds, copyright © 1958 by Helen D. Olds and Harold Berson. Reprinted by permission of Alfred A. Knopf, Inc.

THE MACMILLAN COMPANY: *Lonesome Little Colt* by C. W. Anderson, copyright © 1961 by C. W. Anderson. Reprinted by permission of The Macmillan Company.

WILLIAM R. SCOTT, INC.: *I Know a Farm* by Ethel Collier, copyright © 1960 by Ethel Collier. Reprinted by permission of William R. Scott, Inc.

WONDER BOOKS, INC.: *Surprise in the Tree* by Sara Asheron, copyright © 1962 by Sara Asheron.

THE WORLD PUBLISHING COMPANY: *Benny's Flag* by Phyllis Krasilovsky, copyright © 1960 by Phyllis Krasilovsky.

To children for their first adventures into reading,
here are stories that are not too hard.

Compiled by the
Child Study Association of America

Read-to-Me Storybook
Read Me Another Story
Read Me More Stories
Holiday Storybook
Read to Yourself Storybook
More Read to Yourself Stories
  Fun and Magic
Castles and Dragons
  Read-to-Yourself Fairy Tales
  for Boys and Girls
Read to Me Again
Now You Can Read to Yourself

Contents

Now You Can

Read to Yourself

The Silver Button

BY HELEN D. OLDS

Stevie was in the first grade. He had been in the first grade for three whole days.

The school was three blocks away.

The first day, his mother took him.

The second day, his sister Susan took him. She was ten years old.

Then his mother said, "Today, you can go to school by yourself, Stevie."

Stevie didn't say anything. He

stopped eating his breakfast. He left the table and went out into the hall. Susan was standing before the mirror.

"*You* take me again, please," he said to Susan.

Susan did not answer. She looked at Mother. Stevie looked at Mother, too.

Then Mother said to Susan, "You take him to school this one more time." She smiled. "And he can come home by himself!"

Stevie felt like crying. But he was six years old, so he did not cry.

Susan had her schoolbooks and pencils and pad. But she kept looking for something else. Finally she said, "Come on, Stevie," and she smiled, too.

Stevie went through the hall. He saw his button cap on the table. The cap had buttons all around the rim. Stevie liked to save buttons. He liked

2

his button cap. But he could not wear it to school.

Mother went to the door, too. She waved to them as they started out.

Susan could walk faster than Stevie. "Hurry up," she said. "You are a baby! You *could* go alone."

Stevie did not say anything. He really wanted to go alone. But there were so many fierce things along the way.

In the first block, there was a big brown dog. His name was Trooper. Sometimes he was tied on a long rope. Sometimes he wasn't. Today he was.

Trooper looked as though he might bite. But he didn't. Probably because Susan was there.

"He looks fierce," Stevie said as they went on.

"He's nice," Susan said.

In the next block, there was a big boy. His name was Butch. He was bigger than Susan. He had black hair that was flat on top. He had a red ball in his hands.

Butch aimed the ball right at Stevie. "Watch out, Stevie," he said. "I'll hit you." But he did not throw the ball. Probably because Susan was there.

"He looks fierce," Stevie said as they went on.

"He's *not* nice," Susan said.

In the last block, there was a policeman. They did not know his name. He was so tall and his hands were so big that Stevie felt afraid. The policeman looked cross, too. But he did not scold. Probably because Susan was there.

"He looks fierce," Stevie said as they went across.

"He's nice," Susan said.

Stevie did not say anything. He was thinking about the brown dog, the big boy, and the tall policeman. They all looked fierce. And Stevie would have to pass them when he went home!

Stevie and Susan were at school. Susan let go of Stevie's hand. But she did not rush off. She held out her hand. On it was a silver button. It was about as big as a half-dollar. The button had a lion's head on it.

"Stevie, this is a special button," Susan said. "It will help you to go home alone. And you won't be afraid."

Stevie said, "I like buttons. Thanks, Susan."

Susan pinned it on Stevie's shirt. Then she left him. He went to the play

6

yard. He didn't feel brave yet. Maybe it took time for the button to work.

In the play yard the children shouted and laughed and made noise. All the first-graders were there. And a new girl was there, too. Her name was Amy Beth. She wore a new dress. Her doll wore a matching dress. She asked Stevie, "Did you come to school alone?"

Stevie wished he could say yes. He did not say anything.

Just then Miss Meade called, "Time to come in, children." Miss Meade was the first-grade teacher. Stevie liked her. He liked school, too. Soon he forgot about being afraid.

When school was over, Miss Meade called Stevie to her desk.

"Stevie," she said. "Will you take Amy Beth home? She lives near you."

"Yes," said Stevie. "I will."

He started over to Amy Beth. Then he stopped. He took off the silver button and slipped it into his pocket.

"Come on, Amy Beth," he said. "I'm going to take you home."

"Fine!" said Amy Beth. "I live next to Mrs. Murphy. She has a big brown dog. His name is Trooper."

They started out. Stevie was afraid, but he did not want Amy Beth to know it. He tried not to think about the policeman, and Butch, and Trooper. He and Amy Beth had to pass all three. And Susan wouldn't be there.

At the corner he took Amy Beth's hand. They waited for the policeman's whistle. The button in Stevie's pocket pricked him and he remembered to be brave. He smiled at the tall policeman.

"I'm taking Amy Beth home," he
said.

"Fine," said the policeman. "I've
never had a good look at you. In the
mornings, the sun is in my eyes. It
makes me squint."

9

That was why he looked so fierce in the mornings! Stevie wasn't afraid of the policeman any more. He's my friend, Stevie thought.

The big boy Butch was next. There he was with the red rubber ball in his hands. He aimed the ball right at Stevie. "Watch out," he said. "I'll hit you."

And he threw the ball. But it didn't hit Stevie because it was on a long piece of rubber. The ball snapped right back into Butch's hand.

Butch laughed. Stevie did not laugh. But he wasn't afraid of Butch any more.

Then Butch stuck out his foot and tripped Stevie. Down went Stevie on the sidewalk. He wasn't hurt, but he was angry. He got up and gave Butch a push. "You're not nice," he said.

Then he grabbed Amy Beth's hand and
they rushed on.

Butch called after them, "Stevie,
you're a sport. I like you." He was
smiling.

But Stevie did not turn back. He was thinking about the brown dog. He hoped that Trooper would be asleep.

But Trooper was not asleep. He was not tied, either. He came bounding up to Amy Beth. He put his dusty paws on the front of her new dress. He looked up into her face.

Amy Beth backed away. She held her doll high.

Trooper jumped for the doll. He grabbed it with his mouth. Then he ran with it to his own house.

Amy Beth cried, "My dolly! My poor dolly! Stevie, save her!"

Stevie did not know what to do. Trooper looked fierce. But Stevie had to do something. So he said in a loud voice, "Trooper, give back that doll. Trooper, you are a bad dog."

12

The door of the house opened and Mrs. Murphy came out. She had heard what Stevie said. "Oh, Trooper isn't bad," she said. "He just wants to play. He will give the doll back if you ask him in a friendly way."

"Give it back, please Trooper," Stevie said and held out his hand. He was still a little scared.

The big dog came slowly down the path. He put the doll into Stevie's hand. His wet mouth tickled.

Stevie handed the doll to Amy Beth. He said, "She isn't hurt at all."

"Oh, Stevie, you saved her," Amy Beth said, and she smiled.

Then Mrs. Murphy gave Trooper a small rubber doll and said, "Here's your toy, Trooper."

The big dog took the toy. He rubbed against Stevie's legs.

Mrs. Murphy said, "He likes you. He wants you to pat him."

Stevie reached out his hand and patted Trooper's rough brown head. My, Trooper was nice!

"He likes children. He would never bite anyone," Mrs. Murphy said. "But you are a smart boy, Stevie, to be a little afraid of strange dogs. Remember,

14

all dogs aren't as friendly as Trooper."

Stevie gave Trooper a good-by pat, and he and Amy Beth went on.

Amy Beth's house was next. She said, "Thank you, Stevie, for saving my dolly. And thank you for bringing me and my dolly home."

"It was fun," Stevie said, and he meant it.

"I was so scared," Amy Beth said in a soft voice. "I guess boys aren't *ever* afraid."

Stevie said, "Well, hardly ever." Suddenly he remembered the silver button Susan had given him. He knew it wasn't really magic. But maybe it had helped him to be brave. He said good-by to Amy Beth and raced the rest of the way home.

Mother was waiting for him in the kitchen. She had a peanut-butter sandwich and a glass of milk ready for him.

"You came home all alone!" she said, and she sounded happy. "Daddy will be so proud of you."

"I brought Amy Beth home, too," Stevie said as he sat down at the table. "Susan doesn't have to take me any

16

more. I can go by myself." He thought of the silver button.

Just then Susan came in. She dropped her schoolbooks on the table beside Stevie. "You got home all right?" she asked. She sounded surprised.

Stevie couldn't answer. His mouth was too full. But he nodded his head. The silver button must have helped, he thought.

Susan said, "Look what I found in front of Butch's house." She held out her hand. On it was Stevie's silver button with the lion's head.

Stevie stared at the button. He felt in his pocket. It was empty. He said, "You mean, I didn't have the button? I came home without it?"

He was thinking hard. Then he said, "I didn't need the silver button. I really didn't. I was brave all by myself."

Stevie took the button from Susan. Then he jumped up and ran for his button cap. He pinned the silver button on the very top.

It looked nice. He was going to keep the button to remind him of how brave he could be.

Tim Tadpole and the Great Bullfrog

BY MARJORIE FLACK

Once there was a small pond at the edge of a wood. In the wintertime this pond was very still, but in the springtime these sounds came from the pond.

"Sing-sing-sing-sing!" trilled the tiny Peeper Frogs.

"Jump-come jump-and jump!" croaked the Great Bullfrog.

But there was someone who lived in this pond who could neither sing nor

19

jump and this was a small tadpole named Tim. All day long and all night long Tim Tadpole would listen and listen at the bottom of the pond and feel sorry for himself because he could neither sing nor jump.

Now one warm day as Tim Tadpole was wriggling in and out among the water-lily plants whom should he meet but Mr. Turtle.

"Where are you going, Mr. Turtle?" asked Tim.

"To sit in the sun," said Mr. Turtle, and up and away he swam. Then Miss Salamander came swimming by.

"Where are you going, Miss Salamander?" asked Tim.

"To sit in the sun," said Miss Salamander, and up and away she swam.

Along came the Great Bullfrog.

"Oh, where are you going, sir?" asked Tim.

"To sit in the sun!" said the Great Bullfrog, and up and away he swam.

So Tim Tadpole followed after the Great Bullfrog. Up and up swam the Great Bullfrog and up and up swam Tim.

But the Great Bullfrog climbed up on the mossy bank and poor Tim could not follow after him because he had no legs and no arms to climb with.

Tim Tadpole was left alone with only the snails and little fishes and they were not his friends. So now every day, all day long, Tim Tadpole felt sorry for himself because he could not find the sun. And every night, all night long, Tim felt sorry for himself because he could neither jump nor sing.

One evening just after day and just before night as Tim Tadpole lay in the mud doing nothing whatever but feeling sorry for himself, along came the Great Bullfrog.

"Jump come jump!" said the Great Bullfrog.

"I can't jump and I can't sing and I can't find the sun," said Tim and he began to cry.

"What *can* you do?" asked the Great Bullfrog.

"Swim, just swim," said Tim.

"Then swim!" said the Great Bullfrog, and away he went.

23

So all day long Tim swam and he swam, and all night long Tim swam and he swam, and he never had time to feel sorry for himself at all.

One day what should Tim find kicking out near his tail but two little legs! Then came a day when Tim had a left arm, and then a day when out came a right arm. And every day Tim's tail was getting shorter and shorter and his mouth was growing wider and wider.

"Now," said Tim, "I will find the sun."

Up crawled Tim out of the pond into the air, BUT there was a strange creature looking for his supper. DOWN came his big bill and — SPLASH — back into the pond slid Tim. And away he swam from the Great Blue Heron JUST IN TIME.

24

At last came a day when Tim found he had no tail at all, no tail whatever and his two arms and his two legs were big and strong. Then Tim knew he was no longer Tim Tadpole because he was TIM FROG.

Up and up swam Tim, up he climbed onto the top side of a water-lily pad. And then Tim saw the great ball of a sun, slipping down behind the tall trees.

"Sing-sing-sing-sing," trilled the gay Peeper Frogs.

"I want-to-jump — I want-to-jump," sang young Tim Frog in his little new voice.

"Then jump — come jump — and jump," croaked the Great Bullfrog.

And TIM JUMPED!

Too Many Bozos

BY LILIAN MOORE

"Mother," said Danny Drake. "May I have a dog?"

Danny's mother looked at Danny. "Danny Drake," she said. "You asked me that last week. And what did I say?"

"No," said Danny.

"You asked me that the week before," said his mother. "And what did I say?"

"No," said Danny.

Danny's mother said, "No! I'm sorry, Danny. Our house is too small for a dog."

"But I have a good name for a dog," said Danny. "I want to call him Bozo."

"NO, Danny!" said his mother. And Danny knew it was time to stop.

Danny ran out to the park to play. He played in the park all morning with his friend, Pete. They played they were pirates on a pirate ship. The little brook in the park was a great river. Up and down the river went the pirates in their ship.

Danny saw the little frog first. He knew at once he wanted *that* frog for a pet. Pete helped him catch it. They found a box and put the frog in it. Then Danny carried the frog home.

"Oh, boy!" Danny said to the frog. "Am I glad I found you. Won't Mom be surprised!"

Mom *was* surprised. Danny held up the frog. "Now I have a pet," he told his mother. "Do you want to hold him?"

"No, thanks," said Danny's mother.

"I'm going to call my pet Bozo,"

29

Danny said. "Bozo. Bozo the Frog."

"Please tell Bozo the Frog to stay in *your* room," said Danny's mother.

Danny kept Bozo the Frog in his room and took good care of him. He made a nice home for him and gave him bits of meat to eat.

What fun the frog was! And what a good jumper! First Danny put down one book. Bozo jumped right over it. Danny put down two books, then three. And Bozo jumped over them all.

One day Bozo made one jump too many. The door to his house was open. Jump! Bozo was out of his house. Jump! Jump! He was out of Danny's room. Jump! Jump! Jump! He was here and there, all over the house.

At last Bozo found the best place of all. It was a place with water, so he jumped right in it. He was in the kitchen sink. The sink was full of dishes. Bozo sat on Mother's best green dish.

Danny's mother came in to do the dishes. She screamed when she saw Bozo. Bozo was so scared he jumped out of the sink, right at Danny's mother! "A frog in my sink! Ugh," cried his mother. "Danny, take that frog out of the house at once."

Sadly Danny put Bozo into the box and walked back to the park. On the way he met his friend Billy. "Look what I have," said Billy. He held up a little cage.

"Look what I have!" said Danny. He opened the box a little.

Right then and there — they swapped. Billy took the box and Danny took the cage.

Danny ran all the way home. "Oh,

boy," he said to himself. "Am I glad
I met Billy. Won't Mom be surprised!"

Mom *was* surprised. Danny held up
the cage for her to see. There was a
little white mouse in it.

"This is my new pet," Danny said.
"I'm going to call him Bozo. Bozo the
Mouse." Danny took the mouse out
of the cage and let him hang onto
his sweater. "Look, Mom," he cried.
"See what Bozo does! Do you want
to try it?"

"No, thanks," said Danny's mother.
"And Danny Drake, don't let that
mouse out of your room."

"It's all right, Mom," said Danny.
"Bozo the Mouse won't get in the
sink."

Danny took good care of Bozo the
Mouse. He cleaned Bozo's cage. He
put food and water in it. He played

32

with Bozo every day. Bozo the Mouse
did not get into the sink.

But one morning he got out of his
cage. He got out of Danny's room.
And he went down to the kitchen.

Sniff, sniff, went Bozo the Mouse.
The kitchen was full of a good smell.
Danny's mother had just made a cake
for the Big Cake Sale. That is, it *was*
for the Cake Sale until Bozo the
Mouse saw it. Bozo the Mouse liked
the cake very much.

When Danny's mother took a good look at her cake, she cried, "My cake! Oh, my lovely, lovely cake!" Then she said, "Danny Drake, take that cake-eating mouse out of the house at once."

Sadly, Danny put Bozo the Mouse into his cage. "The best place to take Bozo the Mouse," thought Danny, "is back to the pet shop. That's where Billy got his white mouse in the first place."

So Danny took Bozo to the pet shop. The pet shop man was glad to get the white mouse back.

Danny and the pet shop man made a swap. Danny ran all the way home.

"Oh, boy!" he said to himself. "Am I glad I went to the pet shop! I wonder what Mom will say when she sees what I have now."

Danny's mother did not say anything at first. She just looked at the box Danny was holding. "What in the world is that?" she asked.

Danny held up the box. "This is an ant farm," Danny told her. "See all those ants? I can watch them work and everything."

"Ants!" cried Danny's mother, "I can just see ants all over the house. No ants, Danny Drake. And I mean it."

"Mother," said Danny Drake at last, "I just *have* to have some kind of pet."

"Yes," said Danny's mother. "I can see that you do!" She put her arm

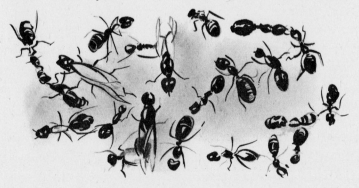

around Danny. "I know just the pet for you," she said.

"Is it better than a frog?" asked Danny.

"Much better," said his mother.

"Is it better than a white mouse?"

"Much, much better," said his mother.

"Is it better than an ant farm?"

"Oh, yes," said his mother. "Much, much, much better. Danny Drake," she said. "How would you like a dog?"

"A DOG," cried Danny, "A DOG!"

"A little dog," said Danny's mother, "because our house is little. But a real dog."

"Oh, boy!" said Danny, "A dog! And guess what I'm going to call him," said Danny. "Bozo. Bozo the Dog."

"Bozo," said Danny's mother. "What a surprise!"

36

Lonesome
Little Colt

BY C. W. ANDERSON

On a farm in the country there were many, many ponies of all sizes and colors. They were all beautiful, with long flowing manes and tails. Each one had a little colt, and they all lived happily together.

Each little colt stayed close beside its mother.

Bluebell was a gray pony. Her colt was red-gold, and she was very proud of him.

Calico's colt was bigger than the others, with long slim legs, and she was very proud of *him*.

Goldie had a lovely little colt of a light-gold color, and she was *very* proud of him. When the flies were very thick, she always brushed them off her colt with her long silky tail. It

made the colt very happy to know
that his mother was always thinking
of him.

But there was one little colt who
had nobody to be proud of him. His
mother had died, and he got his milk
from a bottle each day.

He tried to stand close to Bluebell,

but her colt kept him away. The colt did not want any other colt near her.

One day he stood very close to Bluebell as she and Goldie rubbed each other's backs. He was very happy and felt almost as if he had two mothers. But the colts saw him and chased him away.

When the little colt tried to come near Calico, her colt saw him and kept him away.

Then the little colt thought that the dog, Spot, might be his friend. But Spot saw another dog and ran to join him.

The little colt felt very sad and lonely. All the other colts had mothers and he had nobody.

But two children on the farm had seen how lonesome the little colt was. Mary said to Tommy, "We must be

40

very nice to that little colt that has no mother."

They petted the little colt and played with him. "What a nice little colt," they said. Now he was much happier.

Every day Tommy and Mary came to see the little colt. As soon as he saw them, he came running. Now he felt that somebody really liked him.

When Tommy and Mary petted the little colt, the others came around too, but the lonesome little colt got the most petting.

But Tommy and Mary noticed that even the smallest colt would not let the lonesome little colt come near his mother.

"He misses his mother so," said Mary. "We must tell Daddy about it. Maybe he can think of something we

41

can do for that lonesome little colt."

A few days later the children saw their father drive into the yard. Then he opened the door of the trailer and led out a little pony. She was the color of gold and the most beautiful pony they had ever seen. "She lost her colt when it was born," he said. "Maybe she will like to be a mother to our lonesome little colt."

The little colt whinnied when he saw her and hurried over to her. The lovely pony whinnied back to him.

The beautiful pony nuzzled the little colt softly when he stood beside her. Now there was no one to chase him away. He had a mother of his own.

The little colt stayed so close to his new mother's side that he was like her shadow. She was so beautiful and gentle that he was very proud of her. And

42

he knew from her kind ways that she was proud of him.

Now, at last, he belonged to some-body.

Andy and Mr. Wagner

BY GINA BELL

Andy Brooks sat on the front steps thinking. He was thinking about a dog because he wanted a dog.

Andy had wanted a dog for a long time. And he knew exactly what kind of dog he wanted.

His dog would be a beautiful dog, not too big and not too little. He would have large brown eyes and a reddish-brown coat. Best of all, he would have a long fluffy tail.

Andy even had a name for his dog. He would be called Mr. Wagner, after the fat, jolly man who owned the toyshop.

Suddenly Andy jumped up and ran into the house.

"Mother!" he called. "When can I have Mr. Wagner?"

Mrs. Brooks looked at Andy. "I don't have time to take care of a dog now. When your baby sister Susie is older, I'll have more time. Then maybe you can have your dog."

"But I'll take care of my dog," Andy said. "I'll take care of him all by myself."

"Well, we can't be sure of that," said Mrs. Brooks. "You will just have to wait."

"May I go down to the pet store and look at the dogs?" Andy begged. "May

45

I go see if Mr. Wagner is there now? Susie's getting bigger every day!"

"All right, run along," his mother said. "But don't stay too long."

In the pet shop window Andy saw three dogs. He looked first at a small gold-colored dog.

"You're a nice dog," Andy said. "But you're not Mr. Wagner. Mr. Wagner will be reddish-brown. And he'll be bigger than you."

Next Andy looked at a black dog.

"You look like a smart dog," Andy said. "But you're not as smart as my Mr. Wagner. Mr. Wagner will be the smartest dog in the whole world."

The last dog in the pet shop window was a big reddish dog.

"You're not Mr. Wagner," Andy told him. "You're almost the color of Mr. Wagner, but Mr. Wagner's tail

46

will be longer and fluffier than yours."

Andy sighed as he started home. "I wish I could have Mr. Wagner soon," he said to himself.

He was still thinking about Mr.

Wagner when a little dog ran up to him. A little yellow dog with black spots and a short stump-of-a-tail.

"Hello, doggie," Andy said and kept right on walking. Soon he was in his own front yard.

"Andrew!" It was his mother calling. She was standing by the front door. "Andrew Brooks, where did you get that dog?"

"What dog?" Andy asked.

"That little yellow and black dog behind you," his mother answered.

Andy looked around. There behind him was the little yellow and black dog, wagging its stump-of-a-tail.

"I don't know where he came from," Andy said. "I saw him down the street. He must have followed me home."

"Send him away," said Mrs. Brooks. "He can't stay here."

"Go on," said Andy. "Go on home. You're not my dog. No sir, you're not my Mr. Wagner. Go on home."

The dog looked at Andy. Then it turned and went off down the street.

The next morning as Andy walked to school he was thinking about Mr. Wagner. It seemed as if his beautiful dog were right beside him.

Suddenly Andy looked down. A dog *was* right beside him. But it was the little yellow and black dog. Its stump-of-a-tail was wagging back and forth.

Andy smiled at the dog. "You are a nice little dog," he said. "But you're not mine. Go on home." Andy walked on without looking back.

At the corner near the school, Mike, the policeman, stopped him.

"I didn't know you had a dog, Andy," he said. "You really should feed him more. He looks hungry."

Andy looked down.

"That's not my dog," he said. "I want a dog, but I don't have one yet. My dog is going to be beautiful. He'll be reddish-brown, and he'll have a long fluffy tail."

"That dog's no beauty," the policeman said. "But he acts as if he's your dog."

"I know," said Andy. "But he's just following me."

When Andy had crossed the street, he looked down at the little dog.

"You do look hungry," Andy said. He opened his lunch box and took out a cookie.

"Here," he said. "Here is a cookie for you."

The little dog ate the cookie. Then it looked up at Andy and wagged its stump-of-a-tail.

"Now, I have to go to school, and you have to go home. Go on." Andy hurried toward school.

"Andrew Brooks!" exclaimed the

teacher as Andy came into the room. "Since when do we bring our dogs to school?"

Andy looked around. The little yellow and black dog was trotting behind him.

"He isn't my dog, Miss Smith," said Andy. "He just followed me here."

"Well, he seems to think he's your dog," said Miss Smith. "Please take him outside."

Andy took the little dog to the door.

"Go home," he said.

The little yellow and black dog looked up at Andy. Then it started slowly up the street.

After school Andy walked home with his two friends Bob and Steve. On the way he told them about Mr. Wagner.

"My Mr. Wagner will be beautiful," he said. "And he will be waiting for me every day when I come home."

Soon the boys reached Andy's yard. Up dashed the little yellow and black dog, wagging its stump-of-a-tail. It jumped up and down. It barked. It ran round and round.

"Is *that* your Mr. Wagner?" Bob asked.

"No, *he's* not my dog. I don't know whose dog he is."

"Maybe he doesn't belong to any-one," Steve said as the little dog sniffed at their feet.

"Maybe he doesn't," said Andy thoughtfully.

54

When the boys had gone, Andy and the little dog chased each other around the yard. Suddenly the dog picked up something in its mouth. Andy ran to see what it was. But the little dog was too fast for him. It raced to the porch and laid the something down.

"Mother, Mother!" Andy called. "The little dog found your glove."

Mrs. Brooks came to the door.

"Why, so he did," she cried. "I've been looking for that glove all week. I must have dropped it in the yard. It was smart of the little dog to find it.

"Do you know, Andy, that dog looks hungry. Give him something to eat. There's stew left from last night."

Andy went to the kitchen. He put the stew into a small dish and took it outside.

As soon as Andy put the dish down, the dog ran to it. In a few minutes the stew was all gone.

"Now, do send him away," Mrs. Brooks said. "He can't stay here."

"I'll try," said Andy. "But he seems to think he belongs here."

"Send him away," said Mrs. Brooks.

"Go on!" Andy told the little dog. Slowly the dog walked off.

That evening the doorbell rang. Andy went to see who was there. On the porch stood Mr. Peters, their neighbor.

"Keep that dog of yours tied up,"
he said sharply. "He was digging in
my garden."

"I don't have a dog," said Andy. "I
want one. But I don't have one yet."

"I mean that little yellow and black dog!" Mr. Peters said. "I see him around here all the time."

"Oh, him," said Andy. "He's not my dog. Really he isn't."

"Well, I don't care who he belongs to," said Mr. Peters, turning away. "Keep him out of my garden."

"That dog again," sighed Mrs. Brooks. "I don't know what we are going to do."

"I can't make him go away," answered Andy.

Mr. Brooks looked up from his paper. "We must do something about that dog!"

The next morning while the Brooks family was eating breakfast, the milkman called to them. "Nice dog you have there," he said. "Good size, too. Small."

58

Andy and his mother went out on the porch. "You're right," Mrs. Brooks said. "He is nice and small."

"Friendly little fellow, too," added the milkman as he walked away.

Mrs. Brooks looked at Andy. "What are we going to do with this dog? He just will not go away."

"I think he likes the way you cook beef stew," said Andy. "He's a smart dog."

The little yellow and black dog looked up at Andy and wagged its stump-of-a-tail.

"He seems to know what we're saying," said Mrs. Brooks. "He *is* smart. He found my glove yesterday."

"Yes," said Andy. "And he *thinks* he's my dog."

"Well—well—maybe he can be your dog," said Mrs. Brooks. "Maybe you should have a dog, Andy. Will you take care of him all by yourself?"

"Oh, yes, yes," said Andy. "I'll love him and be good to him. You'll never have to do a thing for him."

Andy grabbed the dog and hugged him tight. The little dog's tail wagged back and forth. It went so fast that Andy could hardly see it.

"What are you going to call him?" asked Mrs. Brooks, laughing at them both.

"Why, Mr. Wagner, of course," said Andy. "I always said I'd call my dog Mr. Wagner."

Mr. Wagner snuggled close to Andy. Back and forth, back and forth, wagged his little stump-of-a-tail.

Peep-Lo

BY JANE CASTLE

Jill's family had a summer cabin at the beach.

Sometimes she waded in the water. Sometimes she played in the sand. Sometimes she hunted for treasure.

One day she saw a big, beautiful shell and ran to pick it up. Just then a bird cried out, "Peep-lo. Peep-lo."

"Where is that bird?" Jill wondered, and looked around.

There it was! It was a plover.

"Peep-lo," it cried again. It seemed to be hurt, for it was dragging one wing in the sand.

"Poor, poor plover," said Jill. "Let me take you to our cabin. Mother and I will fix your hurt wing."

The plover tried to get away from Jill. It even tried to fly with only one wing. Jill ran after it. Once she almost

caught it. But as soon as she put her hand out for it, it flew away. And with both wings too!

"Now, that is funny," said Jill. "You seemed to be hurt, but you can fly all right."

She started to go back for the beautiful shell. But the plover would not let her! It made more cries and flew in her way to stop her.

"My, how angry you act!" Jill called out. "What are you so angry about?" She had to step to one side to get away from the bird. And then she saw a nest.

It had one — two — three — four eggs in it.

Jill laughed. "So you have a secret," she said. "That is why you tried to fool me."

The plover cried at her to go away from the nest.

"I won't hurt your pretty eggs," Jill said. "But now it's my turn to fool you, Mrs. Plover."

Jill ran back to the cabin. Her father let her have his field glasses. Then she crept into the bushes with the field glasses. She lay very still. She whispered, "Now I can watch you and your nest, Mrs. Plover. But you can't see me."

The field glasses made the nest seem

near, near enough to touch. Soon the mother bird flew away. But something was happening to one of the eggs. It was beginning to crack open. The crack in the shell got bigger. The chick inside was hatching.

The little chick pushed and pushed and pushed to get out. It pushed until the egg cracked into two pieces.

The little chick was very wet all over. It had spots like its shell. And it was very tired from all this work. So the chick rested in the sun. The sun dried it and made its fuzz fluffy.

Soon it began to kick so hard that it rolled over in the sand. It opened its tiny bill as it panted for breath.

Now the chick began to hop. It tried to get in the cool shade of the grass. Nearer and nearer to Jill the chick hopped. Hopped and fell over. Jill crept to meet the brave little baby. When it got up to her, it fell against her arm.

Ever so gently Jill touched the baby. It felt soft and warm. "Peep! Peep!" it cried very loudly.

"Peep-lo," its mother answered. She was flying around in wide circles above Jill. Then the mother bird dived down at Jill's head. Again and again she dived down at Jill.

Jill ran away from the plover. Away from the bushes. Away from the darling chick. The mother bird did not follow.

A little later Jill went back slowly and got her shell. It was even more beautiful than she thought it would be.

Through the field glasses Jill saw the plover sitting on her nest again. One wing was spread. Under that wing was her baby safe as could be. It was for her to keep and nobody else could have it.

Stevie Finds a Way

BY RUTH LIEBERS AND
LILLIAN ROTHENBERG

Crash! Bang! Boom!

Stevie West opened his eyes.

What's that, he thought. What's that noise?

Crash! Bang! Boom!

There it was again.

Stevie jumped out of bed. He ran to the window.

"Dad, Dad, come here," he shouted. "Hurry, Dad, hurry."

70

Mr. West ran into the room. "What's the matter?" he asked.

"Oh, now it's too late," Stevie cried. "You can't see it anymore. It's behind the fence."

"What's behind the fence?" asked Mr. West.

"A big power shovel. It just went into the lot on the corner. Look, Dad, look! Now that big dump truck is going in."

"Oh," said his father, "they must be going to build an apartment house."

"Boy, I want to watch that!" said Stevie.

Mr. West laughed. "Lucky you," he said. "I'd like to see it, too, but I've got to go to work."

Stevie had never dressed so fast before.

While he ate breakfast, he told his

mother about the new apartment house.

"You should have seen that dump truck. And there's a power shovel, too. I wonder how it picks up dirt. I wonder how it fills a dump truck.

"I want to watch everything it does. May I, Mom?"

His mother smiled. "Yes," she said. "But don't get in the way."

As soon as he had finished eating,

Stevie ran outside. He hurried to the corner. Policeman Bill waved to him. "Hi, Stevie," he called. "Where are you going in such a hurry?"

Stevie pointed to the lot. "I'm going to see what they're doing."

But when he got there, he stopped. All he could see was the fence around the lot. He looked all around. But wherever he looked, he saw that same fence.

"It didn't look so high from my window," Stevie said to himself. "I can't see a thing. But there must be some way I can watch. There must be some place I can stand."

Just then a dump truck came out from behind the fence. Where did that come from? Stevie wondered.

He ran down the sidewalk. At the end of the sidewalk was a fence. At the end of the fence was a gate. Stevie peeked around the fence and looked through the gate.

"This is good!" he shouted. "I can see everything from here."

The arm of the great shovel went up, up, up. Then it began to swing toward the dump truck.

"Slow, slow, or you'll spill the dirt," Stevie said.

The arm moved slowly.

74

"Just a little more," Stevie said. "Now! Drop the dirt."

The big jaws of the bucket opened, and the dirt tumbled into the truck.

Stevie smiled.

"Hey, kid! Get out of the way," said a loud voice behind him.

Stevie turned around and saw a big man in overalls.

"You can't stay here. You'll get hurt," the man went on. "Besides, I'm the foreman here. One foreman on this job is enough."

Stevie's face got red. "I was only watching," he said.

"This isn't a safe place," said the foreman. "It isn't safe for you to stand here and watch."

Stevie walked slowly away.

Crash! Bang! came from behind the fence.

75

Stevie stopped to listen. What are they doing now? he wondered.

"That old fence," he muttered, kicking at a stone. He watched as the stone flew right under the fence.

Under the fence! There was a little space under the fence.

Stevie lay down flat on the sidewalk. He wiggled around until he could see.

Now he could watch the power shovel. The big bucket was empty. The jaws were open wide. They moved down, down, down until the teeth bit into the ground.

"What a lot of dirt it picks up," said Stevie.

"Hey, kid!" a voice shouted.

But Stevie did not hear.

The bucket was full now. The arm moved slowly up.

"Hey, kid!" the voice shouted again.

It was the foreman. "You can't stay here," he said. "You're blocking the sidewalk."

Stevie looked up.

A workman was waiting to get by with a wheelbarrow. Behind the workman was Mrs. Parker with her baby. And behind her was Johnny Moore. He was riding his bike and tooting his horn.

Stevie jumped up.

"I didn't know I was holding up traffic," he said, and walked sadly away.

"That old fence," he said to himself. "I wish it would fall down."

Suddenly he saw something. "That's what I need," he cried. "A ladder is just what I need."

Stevie ran toward the ladder. It was leaning against the fence.

"Oh, boy," he said. "I'll see everything now."

But just as he got to the ladder, a workman picked it up and carried it off.

"Oh, no!" cried Stevie.

He could still hear the sound of the power shovel. He could still see the workmen go in and out. But he could not see what was happening behind the fence.

78

He just stood there. "Can't look around it," he said. "Can't see under it. And I can't see over it. What can I do now?" Just then someone called, "Hi, Stevie."

Stevie looked up and saw the mailman.

"Oh, hello," said Stevie sadly.

"What's the matter?" asked the mailman.

"Do you know what they're doing behind that fence?" asked Stevie. "They're starting to build an apartment house. And there's a power shovel, and a dump truck. And I can't see a thing."

"Well," said the mailman. "I'd like to see that myself. Too bad the fence is in the way. But since you can't see, why not help me with the mail. I'm going past your house."

79

"Oh, all right," said Stevie. "I might as well."

They walked down the street together. When they got to Stevie's house, the mailman said, "Here's your mail."

Stevie took the mail and ran into the house.

"What are you doing home so early?" asked his mother.

"I came home with the mailman," he answered slowly.

"I thought you were watching the men working," said Mrs. West.

"I couldn't see much," Stevie told her. "The fence was in the way."

"That's too bad," said Mrs. West. "But I'm glad you're here. I need some things from the store. Will you get this list of things for me?"

"Well, all right," said Stevie, "I'll

80

go. And I'll take my wagon along."

On the way to the store Stevie passed some men emptying garbage cans into a big garbage truck. But he did not see them. He was thinking about the fence.

He did not say hello to Policeman Bill on the corner. He was thinking about the fence.

He gave the shopping list to the grocer. But he didn't even look at the candy on the shelf. He was thinking about the fence.

The grocer put everything into a big wooden box. Then he put the box into Stevie's wagon. On the way home Stevie was still thinking about the fence.

When he got home, his mother helped him carry the box upstairs.

"What a heavy box," she said.

Stevie looked at the box. He hadn't really looked at it before. It was just what he needed!

"I think I can use this box, Mom," he said. "May I have it?"

Mrs. West smiled. "I guess you can," she said. "But wait until after lunch if you're going out again."

After lunch Stevie put the box into his wagon and started back to the lot.

Will it work? he wondered.

He took the box out and dragged it to the fence. He pushed the box close to the fence and climbed up on it.

He stood as straight as he could. But he could not see.

He stood high up on his toes. But he could not see. He stretched his neck. But all he saw was the fence.

It didn't work. The box did not help a bit.

Stevie sighed. He sat down on the
box and put his head in his hands.

The foreman walked by and Stevie
looked up. This time the foreman
smiled at him. But Stevie could not
smile back.

Everything wonderful was happening on the other side of the fence. And he could not see a thing.

"Can't look over it," he said to himself. "Can't look under it. Can't look around it. I may as well go home."

That night as he got ready for bed, he thought and thought.

"I can't see around it," he said. "I can't look under it. I can't see over it. I can't see through it."

"See through it!" he cried. "That's it. Maybe I can see through it. I can drill a hole with my brace and bit. Maybe the men will let me drill a hole in the fence."

Stevie ran to a shelf and took down his tool box. He took out his brace and bit. It was just what he needed.

Then he jumped into bed, but he was almost too excited to sleep.

The next morning he was up early.

After breakfast he picked up his brace and bit and hurried to the lot.

Where? thought Stevie, looking up and down the fence. Where is the best place for a hole?

Suddenly a loud voice cried, "What are you doing now?"

Stevie jumped. The brace and bit fell to the ground.

Two men came running down the street. One was the foreman. The other was a workman.

"Still trying, I see," said the fore-man.

Stevie could not say a word. Not one word. He turned and walked slowly away.

"Hey, kid!" the foreman called.

Stevie looked back.

The foreman pointed to the ground.

85

"Is this your brace and bit?" he asked.

Stevie nodded. He walked over and picked up the tool.

"What were you going to do?" asked the foreman.

"I was going to ask if I could drill a hole," Stevie said.

86

"Say," said the workman, "you really do want to watch us, don't you?"

Stevie nodded again.

"It seems to me," said the foreman slowly, "that there should be some way a boy could watch a new building go up."

"A hole is not a bad idea," the workman pointed out.

"You're right," agreed the foreman. "A hole is not a bad idea."

"Then you'll let me drill a hole?" shouted Stevie. "Can I really drill a hole?"

"Why not?" asked the foreman. "In fact, I'll even help you."

Stevie held the bit up to the fence. He turned the handle round and round. The bit went down, down into the wood. Soon there was a hole to look through.

87

And there was the power shovel. Stevie saw it dig into the ground. He saw it swing slowly up, up, up over the dump truck.

Crash! The dirt tumbled into the truck.

Then someone tapped Stevie on the arm. It was the mailman.

"I wish I weren't so tall," he said. "If I weren't so tall, I could see, too."

"You can," said the foreman. "If we can drill one hole, we can drill another."

So Stevie drilled a hole higher for the mailman.

The mailman looked until it was time for him to go on with the mail.

As he left, an old lady came up. She tried to look, too. But she was too short. "I wish I were taller," she said. "I'd like to see, too."

"Why, not?" laughed the foreman.
So Stevie drilled another hole a little lower down.

When he was finished, he ran back to his place. But Billy was there.

"Hey," said Stevie, "that's my place. I drilled that hole myself."

"Yes," said Billy, "but I want to look, too."

The foreman looked at the two boys. He pushed his hat back and laughed and laughed.

"It looks as if we have more work to do, Stevie," he said. "We have one place for tall people, and we have one place for middle-sized people. But we need more than one place for children."

The foreman took the brace and bit. In a minute he had drilled another hole. Then he took a piece of chalk from his pocket and began to write on the fence.

Stevie could not see the writing until the foreman stepped back.

Then Stevie saw:

THIS SPACE RESERVED
FOR STEVIE WEST,
FENCE FOREMAN.

"If it were not for you," said the foreman, "no one could see through the fence." Stevie looked at the sign. He looked at the foreman and smiled. He was very, very proud.

Then he took a long, long look through the hole.

91

Now he could see everything.

The power shovel dropped load after load of dirt into a dump truck. When one truck was full, another truck moved up.

Finally Stevie turned to the foreman.

"How much dirt are you going to take out of this lot?" he asked. "When will you start to build that big apartment house?"

"Watch and see," said the foreman. And Stevie did.

I Know a Farm

BY ETHEL COLLIER

I know a farm. One time I went to it with my father. On the way to the farm, I saw a little green hill.

I told my father, "I wish we had time to roll down that little green hill."

My father said, "We can stop the car. Then you can roll down the little green hill." So I did.

Then, on the way to the farm, we

went over some water. In the water I saw a big fish.

I told my father, "I wish we had time to get that fish."

My father said, "We can stop the car. See if you can get a fish."

I went to the water. I had to hold my hand in it a long time. Once a little fish came near my hand! But I did not get it.

My father made a paper boat for the water. The water took it into some woods.

I said, "I wish I could go into the woods with the boat."

But my father said, "We do not have time." So I did not get into any woods.

Then we came to the farm. It was the farm of Mr. and Mrs. Green. First of all, Mrs. Green gave me an apple.

Mr. Green said, "What would you like to see on this farm?"

I said, "I never saw what is in a barn."

The farmer and my father took me to the barn. It was big and gray. It had big doors. They were not open. A little door was open.

Mr. Green said, "See what you can find in the barn."

I went in. In the barn, just a little sun came in. At first I could not see much. I did not see or hear any animals. But there was a good smell. I could tell that there were animals in that barn!

Then a mouse ran by. I know it was a mouse. I have a picture of a mouse. She had some hay and she ran into a little room.

I could hear something. It came

from the room that the mouse ran into. The door was open a little. I went to see what was there.

A horse was there. He was big and black. His back was round. He had a long black tail.

I think the horse could hear me. I could see him turn his head. He had a long face. But I liked the way his eyes were.

So I went into the room. The horse put his head down. I put my hand to his face. I could tell that he wanted my apple.

All at once he took my apple and ate it!

I went back to the big room of the
barn. Way up near the top I could see
some hay. I could climb up to it. The
hay had a good smell. There was a big
hill of it. I could jump in the hay.
And I did.

When I did, I saw a hen fly up. She gave the hen call, "Cut, cut, cut."

The hen would fly a little. Then she would jump a little. That was the way she got down from the hay.

I found the nest the hen came from.

It was a round nest in the hay. It was just as big as the hen.

An egg was in it!

The egg was warm. I think the hen had just put it there. I took the egg to give it to the farmer.

Then I could hear something little in the hay. I found where it came from. It was kittens. It was four kittens in a nest in the hay.

The kittens were gray and black. Their ears and tails were too little. But I could tell that they were kittens. I took a gray one to hold.

Then a big cat came up into the hay with a jump. She did not want me there. I could tell that. I put her kitten back into the nest. She got into the nest and I went back a little way. But then I could not see the kittens.

For a long time I sat in the hay away

from the kittens. I saw a little bird fly
into the barn. He came in like a jet.
He went to the top of the barn.

Way up there, I could see another
nest. The bird went into it.

Then I could hear my father call
me. I had to hold the hen egg in one
hand and climb down from the hay.

In the big room, I saw the mouse.
I know she had a nest with some mouse
children in it. All the little barn

animals had nests. But I could not find the mouse nest. And I could hear my father call me again.

On the way back to the farm house, I saw a little hen house. Hens were in it. I could not see them but I could hear, "Cut, cut, cut!" There was not time to go in.

I went to the farm house. At the back door there was a good smell. It was cake. I told how the horse took my apple.

Mrs. Green said, "Would you like some apple cake?"

I said, "Yes, thank you," and she cut some apple cake for me.

I put my hen egg down. I sat by some flowers and ate the cake. It was warm. I told how I found the egg and how the bird came in like a jet. I told about the kittens.

Then we had to go home. I gave the hen egg to the farmer.

He said, "Keep the hen egg."

I said, "Thank you. I would like some kittens, too, please." But Mr. Green said that the kittens were too little. They had to stay with the big cat.

Then Mrs. Green cut some flowers. They were for me.

I said, "Thank you for the good time on the farm."

They said, "Come back and see us again."

They wanted me to come back!

My father and I got into the car. And then what do you think Mrs. Green said? She told me, "Come back when the kittens are not so little. Then you may take one home with you to keep."

103

Surprise in the Tree

BY SARA ASHERON

Do you think a dog is the best pet of all?

Jerry did not think so. Jerry liked cats. He liked gray cats and black cats and white cats.

The cat he liked best of all lived across the street. She was a big yellow cat, and her name was Amanda.

One day Amanda had kittens. One kitten was all white. Two kittens were gray and white.

104

One of the kittens was just a little yellow ball of fur, just like Amanda. That was the kitten Jerry liked best. And that was the kitten his mother said he could have for his very own.

Jerry told his kitten a secret. "Next to my mother and father," he said, "I think I love you the most."

The kitten just purred, as if to say, "I know."

One day Jerry's mother said, "Guess what your cat makes me think of?"

"I give up," said Jerry.

"A bright new penny!"

Jerry laughed. "Penny! That's what I'll call you," he told his kitten. And that's how Penny got her name.

Penny was a busy kitten. She was into things and under things all the time.

One day Jerry's mother found Penny

in her new hat. "What in the world
will you do next?" she said.

One day Penny fell into the tub
when Jerry was taking a bath. "That
cat!" said Jerry's mother. "She is into
everything!"

Jerry laughed. "She wants to find out about everything," he told his mother.

Every day, when Jerry came home from school, he looked for Penny. And every day, there she was, waiting for him. Every day, after school, they had milk and cookies together.

But one day, when Jerry came home from school, he did not see Penny at the window. "Where's Penny?" he asked his mother.

"I let her out," his mother said. "I guess she has not come back yet."

Jerry ran outside. "Here, Penny," he called. "Here, Penny."

Penny was not in the basket. Penny was not under the steps. Penny was not in the tall grass. Where was his kitten?

Jerry ran down the street. "Here,

107

Penny!" he called again and again. "Here, Penny!"

"Meow!"

Was that Penny?

"Meow!"

Yes, it was his kitten. Jerry looked around, but he did not see her.

"Meow!" cried Penny again.

Jerry looked up. There was Penny, way up in a tree.

"Meow!" cried Penny. "Meow!"

Jerry could see how scared she was. He called up to her, "It's all right, Penny. I'm going for help, and I'll be right back."

Jerry ran up the street to his house. "Mom, Mom," he cried. "Penny is way up in a tree, and she's too scared to come down!"

Jerry's mother went at once to get a ladder. Then she saw the tree. "Oh no,"

she said. "This ladder will never do!"

"Meow!" cried Penny. "Meow!"

"Oh Mom," said Jerry, "she's so scared! I can tell. Do something!"

Jerry's mother looked up at Penny. "I'll call the Fire Department," she said. "They will come and get her down."

Jerry's mother called the Fire Department. "Our kitten is up in a tree," she said. "Can you help us get her down?"

"We will come as soon as we can," the fireman said.

Soon? It did not seem very soon to Jerry. He stood under the tree, feeling more and more unhappy.

"Meow! Meow!" Penny called and called. And it seemed to Jerry that she was calling, "Get me down! I'm scared, up here!"

110

Jerry could not wait. He *had* to help his kitten. He began to climb the tree. "Don't be scared, Penny," he called to her. "Here I come!"

Jerry climbed up as far as he could go. But he could not get up to Penny. And now he could not get down.

Penny looked down at Jerry. She liked having him in the tree. Now she was not so scared.

She stood up and looked around. She looked down at the next tree. She took one step, then another. She jumped into the other tree and ran down.

Clang! Clang! The fire truck was coming down the street.

Jerry's mother ran out to meet the firemen. "This way!" she cried. "Our cat is up in this tree."

The firemen took a big ladder and

ran to the tree. One fireman looked up at the tree.

"Does your cat wear blue jeans?" the fireman asked.

Jerry's mother looked up, too. "Jerry!" she cried. "What are *you* doing up there?"

"I can't get down," said Jerry.

"Meow!" cried Penny.

Jerry's mother looked down. "And what are *you* doing down here?" she said.

"Meow!" cried Penny, "Meow!"

The fireman began to climb the ladder. "I will have to hurry," he said, "before the cat goes up to get the boy who went up to get the cat."

"Hello, Jerry!" said the fireman. "How do you like it up here?"

"Not so very much," said Jerry.

"Hold on, then," said the fireman.

112

"Let's go!" And down the ladder he came with Jerry.

"Thank you!" said Jerry.

"You're welcome!" said the fireman. "It's not every day I climb up to get a cat out of a tree and come down with a boy instead!"

Benny's Flag

BY PHYLLIS KRASILOVSKY

Benny was an Indian boy who lived in Alaska many years before it became a state. He had straight black hair and bright black eyes, but best of all he had the whitest white teeth and a happy, friendly smile.

Everyone liked Benny, for Benny liked everyone. He had no father and mother, but he had many, many friends in the mission home where he lived. That was a place for boys and girls who had no families.

The children ate together in a big dining room. They slept in big rooms which had many beds in them. And in the winter they all went to the same school that the other children in the village attended.

Benny was happy in the mission home. But sometimes before he went to sleep at night, he would gaze at the stars outside his window and long for the day when he would be a grown-up man. For then he was going to be a fine fisherman.

He would use a big net like the Big Dipper to catch splendid silver fish. And like the Big Dipper, which was really a great strong bear of night, he would be big and strong himself. The North Star would guide his boat, for

115

the North Star is the star of Alaska,
the northern most state of America.

Sometimes, when the sky was filled
with stars, it reminded Benny of a

field of forget-me-nots, the little star-shaped flowers which grow wild everywhere. The blue sky was a roof that covered Benny's Alaska at night.

In the summertime, when only the tops of the mountains were still covered with snow, Benny enjoyed himself on picnics with the other mission children. Sometimes he went swimming, too, though the water was often cold.

One lucky day a kind fisherman took Benny fishing with him in his boat. Almost at once Benny caught a big silver salmon all by himself. It was so big that there was enough for everyone at the mission house to eat for supper, and they all said the fish was delicious.

Benny was so happy he could hardly sleep that night. He lay awake looking at the stars, dreaming his dream of becoming a real fisherman.

The Big Dipper looked more than ever like a great strong bear because

Benny felt so big and strong himself.

When fall came, school started again just as it does for children everywhere. But the winter came quickly, far more quickly than it does anywhere else.

The first snowy day Benny went to school wearing a *parka,* which is a fur-hooded jacket, and *mukluks,* which are fur-lined boots, and thick mittens to keep his fingers warm. He looked more like a furry bear than an Indian.

That day in school the teacher told the children that there was a contest to make a flag for Alaska. With all his heart Benny wanted to win the contest. He thought how grand it would be to see his flag carried in a parade or flying at the masts of big ships that came to the village in the summertime. He thought how grand it would be to see his flag flying on the fishing boat he would have one day.

That night the boys and girls at the mission house collected crayons, paints, and paper, and made many, many designs for the flag. They sat around a big table and as they worked they talked and laughed and sometimes held up their designs for the others to see.

But Benny sat quietly, thinking and thinking. For once no one could see

120

his white teeth and happy, friendly smile. He was thinking of what he loved the most about Alaska.

Some of the children drew pictures of the beautiful snow-covered mountains in Alaska. Some drew pictures of the big fish that can be caught in Alaska. Some drew pictures of the northern lights that sometimes cross Alaskan skies. Some drew pictures of the Alaskan forests. Some drew pictures of the Alaskan glaciers, and some drew pictures of the Alaskan rivers.

Suddenly Benny knew what he wanted his flag to be like. He wanted his flag to be like the stars he dreamed by—gold stars spread out like the Big Dipper in the blue sky. So that is what he painted.

Underneath it he wrote: "The blue field is for the Alaskan sky and the forget-me-not, an Alaskan flower. The North Star is for the future state of Alaska, the most northerly of the Union. The Dipper is for the Great Bear — standing for strength."

Benny didn't show his paper to anyone. He was too shy. He thought the other children's designs were much better than his. Still, the next day he gave his paper to the teacher when she collected the others.

A month went by and the teacher did not mention the contest again. Benny ice-skated and had snowball fights and went sleigh-riding with the other children.

And so the winter went quickly.

Suddenly the snow and ice began to melt. Benny no longer wore his *parka* and *mukluks* and mittens. He began to watch for the forget-me-nots in the

drying fields as he walked to school. He watched the fishermen mend their nets for the coming fishing season. He watched the world change from white to green.

Then, one day, when school was almost over, the teacher called the children together. "Children," she said, "the flag contest is ended. From all over Alaska boys and girls sent in designs for the flag. From everywhere came hundreds of designs. And . . .

Boys and girls! *Benny's* design won the contest! From now on, *Benny's* design will be Alaska's flag."

What a proud and happy boy Benny was! And what a very proud and happy boy he was on the Fourth of July. On that day there was a big parade. Everyone came to see the parade, to see the marchers with their drums and fifes, to see the banners.

But the very first thing they saw was BENNY . . . Benny marching at the head of the parade, carrying the flag he had made for the fishing boat he would have, carrying the flag he had made for Alaska.

This is a true story.

What the Moon Is Like

BY FRANKLYN M. BRANLEY

Did you see the moon last night? Was it big and round?

When the moon is round, people say they can see "the man in the moon."

The dark and light parts make them think of a mouth, a nose, and two eyes.

That is why they say there is a man in the moon.

126

Next time the moon is big and round, look at it.

The moon is far away, but we can see it very well.

We see that the moon is round like a ball.

Parts of the moon are bright. Other parts are dark.

Craters look bright. Seas look dark.

These are the bright and dark places you see when you look at the moon.

Make believe you are on the moon. What would it be like?

There is no air on the moon.

You cannot live without air, so you would need a space suit on the moon. There would be air inside the space suit.

If you were in sunlight on the moon, it would be very hot. The space suit would keep you cool.

When you were out of the sunlight, it would be very cold. The space suit would keep you warm.

Do you weigh 60 pounds? You would weigh only 10 pounds on the moon. So would your friend. You could pick him up easily. That's because there is low gravity on the moon.

You could pick up big rocks. You could throw them far, too.

You could jump from place to place.

You could move easily in your space suit. You could jump over a house, if there were houses on the moon.

You could explore the moon mountains. They are high and steep.

You could look into deep valleys. You would see rocks all over.

You could look into deep cracks in parts of the moon.

In the cracks you would see only rock and stone.

Nothing lives on the moon.

You would see no plants, flowers, birds; no grass, no animals.

You could explore the moon craters.

Craters are flat places with hills around them like a wall.

Some craters are little. You could

walk across them. Others are big. One crater is 180 miles wide.

You could jump up the wall of a crater to see the other side.

Maybe you would see a layer of dust so deep you could sink into it.

Maybe you would see a lunar sea.

Lunar seas are big flat places on the moon. We call them seas because they are flat, not because they hold water. There is no water on the moon.

Some of the seas have high walls. If you stood beside them, you would look very small.

We want to know more about the moon.

We send rockets there to gather information and send it to us.

Some day men will go to the moon. They will live inside the rocket that takes them to the moon.

Outside the rocket the men will wear space suits. The space suits will keep them from getting too cold or too hot.

They will take tanks of air with them so they can breathe.

They will take water and food, too.

When men go to the moon, they will explore the mountains, the deep cracks, the craters, and the seas.

They will be moon explorers.

Moon exploring will be exciting.

Some day, you may be a moon explorer.

132

About the Child Study Association of America

The Child Study Association of America is a nonprofit organization. Since 1888 its program has been to help parents bring up their children with wisdom and enjoyment. It works with families through parent discussion groups, lectures, publications, individual counseling and training for professional workers.

The Children's Book Committee of the association carefully reviews all the books currently published for children and issues an annual list for the guidance of parents in selecting books for their children. This story collection and many others, welcomed by parents and children alike, have grown out of the committee's long years of experience in reviewing and in evaluating the appeal of stories to children of all ages.

About the Artist

Peter Burchard was born in Washington, D.C., and was graduated from the Philadelphia Museum School of Art. During World War II he served as a radio operator on a troop transport in the North Atlantic. His first published illustrations appeared in Yank *magazine.*

Mr. Burchard has three children, two girls and a boy. He lives with his wife and family in Rockland County, New York.